Wellie wishers™

A Fin-tastic
Surprise

By Valerie Tripp
Illustrated by Thu Thai

★ American Girl®

Editorial Development: Teri Robida
Art Direction and Design: Jessica Rogers
Production: Caryl Boyer, Tami Heinz, Jodi Knueppel

americangirl.com/service

Not all services are available in all countries.

Parents, request a FREE catalog at **americangirl.com/catalog**.
Sign up at **americangirl.com/email**
to receive the latest news and exclusive offers.

For Teri Robida
with thanks

Meet the WellieWishers

The WellieWishers are a group of fun-loving kids who each have the same big, bright wish: to be a good friend. They love to play in a large and leafy backyard garden cared for by Willa's Aunt Miranda.

Willa

Ashlyn

Emerson

When the WellieWishers step into their colorful garden boots, also known as wellingtons or *wellies*, they are ready for anything—stomping in mud puddles, putting on a show, and helping friendships grow. Like you, they're learning that being kind, creative, and caring isn't always easy, but it's the best way to make friendships bloom.

Kendall

Camille

Bryant

GARDEN MAP

Chicken Coop

Carrot's Hutch

Playhouse

Garden Gate

Aunt Miranda's House

Garden Theater Stage

Greenhouse

Pond

Wild Area

Castle

N
W   E
S

Garden
Shed

Veggie
Garden

Tea Table

Wild Area

Chapter 1

Splishy, Splashy Fun!

One hot and ho-hum day, Camille said, "I know what will perk us up. Let's play mermaids."

"I'll be a mer-boy, and Pegeen can be a mer-pig," said Bryant.

"And we'll *all* be mer-friends," said Willa.

"That sounds like fun!" agreed
the rest of the WellieWishers.

Camille sang to the tune of "Row, Row, Row Your Boat":

Splish, splash, swim so fast,
Underneath the sea!
Make a wish
To be half fish.
Come along with me!

The WellieWishers held hands and
chanted:
Close your eyes, stand in a row,
All hold hands, and off we go!

Once upon a tide, a happy group
of mer-friends lived under the sea.

"Let's race to the reef!" said
Mermaid Camille. "On your mark,
get set, *flow*!"

Swoosh! The mer-friends took off, swimming fast. Their quick, shimmery fish tails were as bright as silver. The mer-friends raced to the coral reef, leaving a trail of bubbles behind them.

"You win!" Mermaid Kendall congratulated Mermaid Emerson. "Here is your prize."

"Hooray!" cheered the other mer-children as Mermaid Kendall slipped a beautiful lei made of pearls, kelp, and seashells around Mermaid Emerson's neck.

"Thank you," said Mermaid
Emerson. She swam and swooped a
loop-de-loop to show how pleased
she felt.

The mer-friends loved their undersea world. They took care of the fragile coral reefs. They freed sea creatures that were tangled up in plastic trash.

They chatted with the friendly dolphins. They cheered up the crabby crabs so that they were as happy as clams.

At night, gentle, giant whales kept watch as the mer-children said good night to the moon smiling down at them. They sang a sleepy song:

Sing, sing, sing along,
Sing a sleepy tune.
Say good night,
To all the stars
And the smiling moon.

Then the mer-children called to
one another, "Good night! I love you!
Sleep well!"

Safely surrounded by their sea-
creature friends, the mer-children
were rocked to sleep by the waves.

Chapter 2

The Beachcomber

"Gee *whale*-a-kers!" Willa exclaimed one morning. "My hair is as tangled as seaweed! It smells fishy, too."

"Let's go to Madame Tresses' beauty salon," said Emerson.

"Yes!" said the other mer-children.

It was always a treat to see
Madame Tresses. Her beauty salon
was called The Beachcomber.

Madame Tresses did it all: She trimmed the whiskers on the catfish and the walrus. She untangled the jellyfish's tentacles. She curled the seahorse's tail, smoothed the gull's feathers, shined up the snail's antennae, polished the turtle's shell, and oiled the clam's hinges—and she still had an arm free to wave hello to everyone who came in.

The Beachcomber

Madame Tresses kept her customers laughing. It was no wonder that The Beachcomber was a popular spot. In fact, it was so popular that it was outgrowing its space. "My customers are packed in here like sardines," Madame Tresses joked. "I *dolphin*-ately need more space."

Sea you soon!

Let's make some *waves*!

25

Madame Tresses finished Willa and Camille first.

"Thank you, Madame Tresses," Camille said. "Willa and I will leave, to make room for your other customers."

"I *shore* do appre-*sea*-ate it!" joked Madame Tresses.

The two mermaids waved goodbye and swam off together.

"I love Madame Tresses, but I hate being crammed into that tiny space," Camille confessed. "I always feel so *squooshed*! Let's go for a nice long swim. I need to stretch my fins."

"Me, too!" said Willa. "Let's go!"

Chapter 3

The Ship

After they had swum for a while, Camille exclaimed. "Oh, look! A ship."

"A ship*wreck,* you mean," said Willa. "Let's explore it."

The old, sunken ship was sad looking. Its masts were broken. Its sails were tattered. Seaweed twisted in and out of its windows. Barnacles clung to the walls. There were heaps of sand in every corner.

"Wouldn't this make the most wonderful clubhouse?" asked Camille.

"Yes!" agreed Willa. "Let's fix it up. When it's ready, we'll bring our mer-friends here. It'll be a—"

"Surprise!" Camille and Willa said together. They hugged.

"Our mer-friends are going to love the clubhouse *and* the surprise!" said Camille.

"That's a *shore* thing!" said Willa. "Everyone loves a surprise!"

Camille and Willa dove right in!
Millions of tiny, shiny fish darted
around them. Slow sea turtles
watched, smiling and nodding, as the
two mermaids worked.

Fixing up the ship to use as
a clubhouse was harder than
they had thought it would be. But
Camille and Willa kept at it. As
they worked, they sang:

Sweep, sweep, sweep, and scrape!
Clear the mess away!
Make the ship the perfect place
For our friends to play.

The next day at the coral reef, the other mer-friends were curious.

Ashlyn asked, "Where did you two go yesterday?"

Willa and Camille were bursting to tell their friends about the ship. It was so hard not to give away their surprise!

"We're working on a project," Camille said. "We can't wait to share it with you! But it's not quite ready yet."

"We want to surprise you when it's all done," Willa explained.

"And looking perfect," Camille added.

"I get it," said Bryant. "You want your surprise to make a big *splash* when it's finished!"

Camille and Willa laughed. "Exactly!" they said.

"Ooooh, that sounds like fun," said Emerson. "I love surprises!"

"Me, too," said Ashlyn. "I hope your project goes *swimmingly*."

"Thanks," said Willa as she and Camille swooshed off.

"Ahoy, Madame Tresses!" the mermaids called on their way to the ship.

The Beachcomber

OPEN

"Ahoy!" answered Madame Tresses, waving.

"The Beachcomber looks jam-packed, as usual," said Camille.

"You mean *jelly*-packed, since there are jellyfish in there!" said Willa with a giggle.

Chapter 4

An Even Nicer Surprise

When the mermaids arrived at the shipwreck, their hearts sank a little.

"The shipwreck is wreckier than I remembered," said Camille.

"And the mess inside is messier," said Willa.

"Well!" said Camille stoutly. "That just means that our nice surprise for our mer-friends is even nicer than we thought it was."

"Right!" said Willa.

The two mermaids shook off their discouragement and went to work. Whenever they began to feel tired, they thought of their mer-friends.

"Our friends are going to be blown away by the clubhouse," said Camille. "All our hard work will be worth it."

She and Willa sang:

Yes, yes, yes, we can!
We'll fix up the ship!
When we spring our nice surprise
All our friends will flip!

Camille and
Willa worked hard
all that day, and
at the end of the
next day . . .

"Perfect!" sighed Willa.

"Almost," said Camille.

"Let's go get our mer-friends!" said Willa eagerly.

"I'm not quite done," said Camille. "But go ahead and gather everybody. I'll follow you as soon I can, and then we can bring our friends here and show them our—"

"Surprise!" both mermaids shouted together.

"Okay," said Willa. "I'll see you in a jiffy. Have fun with your *fin*-ishing touches!" Willa swam off, quick as a fish.

When Camille was finished, she headed back to the coral reef. She passed The Beachcomber on her way.

"Ahoy!" Camille called out to Madame Tresses. But The Beachcomber was so crowded and there was such a long line of customers waiting outside that Madame Tresses didn't see or hear Camille.

Poor Madame Tresses, thought Camille. *She's as squeezed as a snail that's too big for its shell. I wish we could help her somehow.*

Just then, Camille had an idea.

With a mighty swish of her mermaid tail, Camille powered herself forward. She swam as fast as she could. She caught up with Willa just before Willa reached the coral reef. "Wait!" Camille called out.

Willa stopped and turned. "What's up?" she asked.

"Listen," Camille panted. After she told Willa her idea, Camille asked, "What do you think?"

For a second, Willa didn't answer.

Uh-oh! thought Camille. *Willa doesn't like it.*

Then Willa said, "I love it! The clubhouse idea was a nice surprise for our mer-friends, but this will be an even nicer surprise for *all* our friends!"

Chapter 5

A Conspira-*sea* of Kindness

Ready for the surprise?" Camille and Willa asked their mer-friends.

"Yes!" they cheered.

"Then follow us," Camille said. She and Willa led their friends to the ship. On the way, they passed The Beachcomber.

"Look," said Emerson, "the salon is crowded as usual."

Camille and Willa glanced at each
other and smiled.

"*W-h-o-a!*" gasped Ashlyn, Bryant, Emerson, and Kendall when they saw the ship. They explored every inch of it—and they *loved* every inch of it, too!

"What *is* this place?" asked Kendall. "What's it used for?"

"Well," said Camille. "We thought of using it as a clubhouse, but—"

"But then Camille had a much nicer idea," Willa piped up. "Tell them, Camille."

"You know how The Beachcomber is always packed to the gills?" said Camille. "Madame Tresses needs a bigger space. So what if *this* was her salon?"

"Oooooh," cooed Emerson. "That would be ex-*shell*-ent!"

"Let's move Madame Tresses' equipment here as a surprise for her," said Willa.

"Great idea!" said Kendall. "But how will we do it without Madame Tresses seeing us?"

"I have a plan to distract Madame Tresses," said Camille. "It'll take some

fancy *fin*-work! We'll need our sea-
creature friends to help us pull it off."

"I'm sure they'll help," said Ashlyn
confidently. "It will be a conspira-*sea*
of kindness for Madame Tresses."

"Where are my customers?" asked Madame Tresses the next day.

"Oh, Madame Tresses, there's a terrible problem," said Bryant. "Look! They're all in a tangle!"

"Oh, my starfish!" exclaimed Madame Tresses. "That's a whale of a mess!"

"Please come help us," said Camille.

Madame Tresses had to use all of her arms to untangle the sea creatures. She was very focused on her task.

While Madame Tresses worked,
the mer-friends quickly picked up
everything in her salon and swam
off with it.

When everyone was untangled, the walrus pretended to be exhausted.

"Do you think we should call the *clam*-bulance?" Madame Tresses asked.

"No," said Camille. "But we had better help the walrus swim home, to be sure he gets there safely. Follow me. I know the way."

Camille led the way to the ship.

"SURPRISE!" everyone shouted.

"Holy mackerel!" gasped Madame
Tresses. "What's this?"

The Beachcomber

"It's The Beachcomber," Willa said, "in a bigger space. What do you think?"

"I think it's *fin*-tastic!" said Madame Tresses. "Now there will be room for everyone!"

"Thank you, my friends," cried Madame Tresses, wrapping the mer-children into a hug.

"You're *whale*-come!" they answered happily.

Sweet Surprises

It's no secret that kids love surprises. An unexpected item, event, or treat to eat makes an ordinary day special. Here are some fun and easy surprises you can create for your child.

Secret messages

A lunch box is a perfect surprise location, but there are also plenty of places around the house to stash a fun surprise. Put a note in her underwear drawer, by her toothbrush, or in her favorite box of cereal. The more unexpected the better!

Treasure hunt

Play hide-and-seek with a toy! It can be an item she already owns, but it's especially fun with a new toy. Instead of purchasing something, do a toy swap with a friend.

Picnic

Eat in an unexpected place. Your yard or a park are fun outdoor spaces, but you can also have a picnic inside. Give your child a blanket and let her pick the room.

Scavenger hunt

Make a list of items for your kids to find in the house or yard. List specific items or challenge your child to find something that starts with each letter of the alphabet. Have a small prize, such as stickers, bubbles, or a treat to eat, ready when she's finished.

While she's sleeping…

Hang colorful balloons from the ceiling and tape streamers to the top of her door frame. This is a fun way to celebrate a birthday, but it's also a delightful surprise to wake up to any day of the year.

Backward day

Tell your kids that it's Backward Day and ask them to come up with silly ways to do things in reverse. Read a book by starting on the last page. Eat dessert before dinner. Answer the phone by saying "Goodbye." Walk backward around the block. Get creative and have fun!

Surprise treats

Put a bag of fruit snacks in the pocket of her jacket. Hide a granola bar in her backpack. Tuck an applesauce pouch in the cupholder of her car seat. Choose your child's favorite snack and leave it for her to find.

Share delight

Kids are also eager to plan surprises for others. Let your child be the one to create these magical moments for friends or family members. Write ideas on separate pieces of paper. Fold the papers and put them in a bowl. Let your child pick a piece of paper and then carry out the task.

About the Author

VALERIE TRIPP says that she became
a writer because of the kind of person she is.
She says she's curious, and writing requires you
to be interested in everything. Talking is her
favorite sport, and writing is a way of talking
on paper. She's a daydreamer, which helps her
come up with her ideas. And she loves words.
She even loves the struggle to come up
with just the right words as she writes
and rewrites. Ms. Tripp lives in
Maryland with her husband.